ISBN 978-1-959451-02-0

Siohan Press
www.siohanpress.com

Like humans, birds use all five senses - sight, smell, hearing, taste, and touch.

# A Lot Like You:
# BIRDS

## Marilyn D. Williams

A bird's eyes are on the sides of its head so it can see almost all the way around.

A bird's body is lightweight for efficient flying.

Birds flap their wings to take off, soar, and land with skill.

The touch sense is key for birds to feel the air and perch on branches.

Most birds begin each day by singing sweet melodies and chirping.

These cheerful sounds help birds find mates and defend their territory.

Birds use their sense of smell to find food and identify dangers.

The nostrils of birds are located at the base of their beaks.

Birds can hear higher and lower sounds than the human ear.

Hawks and owls have incredible hearing to help them hunt small prey.

Birds do not have a good sense of taste. They rely more on sight and smell to find food.

Some birds can see well at night for hunting after dark.

Birds eat foods like insects, seeds, fruit, and grains.

Hummingbirds sip nectar from flowers using their long tongues.

Some birds soar high in the sky to spot smaller animals below.

Powerful wings and hollow bones make birds excellent aviators.

In fall and winter, many birds migrate long distances in search of food.

Birds that live near oceans or lakes dive into the water to catch fish.

Young birds spend a lot of time playing and exploring their surroundings.

Their playful antics help young
birds practice important life skills.

Birds collect twigs, grass, feathers, and more to build cozy nests.

A bird may spend days or weeks carefully building its home.

Pairs of birds take turns caring for their nest of eggs or hatchlings.

Flocks of birds work together to find food, migrate, and watch for predators.

Like humans, birds enjoy hanging out with other birds for company and fun.

They spend time sitting together on branches and helping each other stay clean.

Birds use calls and gestures to communicate with other birds.

When birds see danger, they raise the alarm by squawking loudly.

Birds love splashing and playing in birdbaths or puddles to stay clean and cool off.

They also take dust baths to remove dirt, oil, and bugs from their feathers.

Birds may seem very different from us, but the things they do show that we are a lot alike.

How similar are you to a bird?

www.ingramcontent.com/pod-product-compliance
Lightning Source LLC
Chambersburg PA
CBHW040438150626
46551CB00023B/111